Leadership: Seeing and Seizing the Opportunity

Jeffrey A. James

ISBN: 978-1-7345851-1-7
Paperback
Library of Congress Control Number
2020941750

Printed in the USA

Table of Contents

CHAPTER 1

New Beginnings

A ll leaders are born the same, regardless of their family, social, economic, or religious status. The one thing we all have in common is that we were all born in sin without ever committing the actual sin. We all needed Jesus' life, death, and resurrection to give us a new beginning.

What does it mean to have new beginnings? I like to look at it this way. A new beginning is a fresh start or a clean slate. It's when you have been given a chance to start over and you accept the offer.

2 Corinthians 5:17

"Therefore if any man be in Christ, he is a new creature: old things are passed away; behold, all things are become new."

When I think of a true leader in the Bible who was given a fresh start and a clean slate, I think of the Apostle Paul. In the book of Acts, Paul, then named Saul, was clearly against Christians and God's church. We also see that after his encounter with Jesus, he changed and began to preach Christ in the synagogues and that Christ was the Son of God.

Acts 9:1 & 2

1 "And Saul, yet breathing out threatenings and slaughter against the disciples of the Lord, went unto the high priest, 2 And desired of him letters to Damascus to the synagogues, that if he found any of this way, whether they were men or women, he might bring them bound unto Jerusalem."

Acts 9:20

"And straightway he preached Christ in the synagogues, that he is the Son of God."

This is what I call a new beginning, a fresh start, and a clean slate! Paul was offered a new beginning by Jesus and he accepted the offer, which changed his life for the better forever.

Jesus has offered us a new beginning, a fresh start and a clean slate. But for us to benefit from it, we must accept the offer and receive Him as Lord. Until we do, we should never be considered for a leadership position. I know this sounds elementary, but there are still plenty of so-called leaders running churches, ministries, and other organizations that are supposed to be Christ-centered. A new beginning with Christ is a prerequisite before becoming a leader in God's Kingdom.

Too many times churches and Christ-centered organizations put people in positions because they have expertise in a certain area. This is a recipe for disaster if the person has not received Jesus as Lord and savior. Asking the potential leader if they have received Jesus as Lord and Savior is not enough. We must see their fruit and monitor their commitment to the Kingdom. If you asked 10 random church attendees if they've received Jesus as their Lord and Savior, I believe most of them would answer with a resounding yes, whether they have or not. Therefore, we must be prayerful and diligent about elevating people to leadership positions without being assured of their salvation. There are some who are saved but have been through the fire and just need a second chance. They also can have a new beginning.

A new beginning for some simply means that they are forgetting the things behind and reaching for those things that are ahead. I've found that often our new beginnings are awaiting our arrival. Waiting for us to forget about what has been and reach for what's ahead. Leaders don't spend their time crying over spilled milk, they make milkshakes. Whatever happened to them in the past is what they use to make their next milkshake tasty. They take full advantage of the opportunities of today and tomorrow. Never allow your yesterday to make you believe that today is its twin. No! Leaders expect every day to be better than the day before. Great leaders choose what type of day they will have before the day ever arrives. Today is your day to choose what your tomorrow will look like, don't waste it.

Have you ever flunked an exam and the instructor gave you an opportunity to retake the exam? How did you feel? Were you excited? Did you thank him/her and tell him/her you will do better this time? This is what it feels like to have a new beginning: excited, grateful, and a commitment to improve. Leaders get excited about a new beginning. They are excited about having another opportunity to succeed and thrive. They are excited about the new challenges they will face and are ready to face them with enthusiasm.

As a leader, your excitement, enthusiasm, and passion are key ingredients that keep you and your followers moving forward when challenges arise. I've come to realize that leaders who lack these key ingredients do more harm for their team than help. If my team doesn't know what to do, I can give them information. If they don't have enough resources, I access more resources to distribute. If my team lacks manpower, I can get them more help, but if they lack excitement, enthusiasm, and passion, we are in for a long bumpy ride and we may not like where we end up. I'd much rather work with people that exhibit excitement, enthusiasm, and passion than to work with someone without it but has a wealth of knowledge. People without excitement, enthusiasm, and passion drain the life out of you. When we allow them to drain us, we make our jobs more difficult, our journey longer, and we lose momentum.

CHAPTER 2

DON'T TRY TO PUT PEOPLE IN SHOES THAT DON'T FIT THEM

O ne trend I've noticed that has become very popular in the church setting is people and leaders are trying to put others in shoes that don't fit them. Do you know how it feels to wear shoes that don't fit properly? I'll answer for you, it's very painful! Here are several signs that your shoes don't fit you properly:

If you must loosen all your laces completely in order to remove them.

This means if menial tasks are like pulling teeth for you and others do them with little to no effort, you may need to change shoes. What you are trying to do may not be what you are supposed to be doing, even if a person of influence elevated you. Please don't misunderstand what I am saying. I'm not saying everything you do should be sweat less, but I am saying there are times that we try to do something because we've been told that's what we are supposed to do and those who told us were wrong. I don't think they missed it on purpose, but regardless of their intent, you feel like you are being choked to death doing something that should come easy to you.

I've seen many couples fall prey to this. One of them feels they are called to ministry, but they feel they must force the other into that role as well. Trying to make someone something they are not is like trying to make a dog a human. You allow the dog to live in your home, you feed him the best food, bathe him, talk to him, take him with you on car rides, you watch

TV together, go for walks, and even call him your baby. There's nothing wrong with this, but it's still a dog and a dog will be a dog and never become anything other than a dog. Why? Because that's what he's supposed to be: a dog. That's what God made it to be and it can be nothing else. The dog can be trained to do some things humans do and may do them well, but it's still a dog. God created him to be a dog and Adam gave him his name and characteristics. Unlike dogs, humans were given their spirit, soul, body, and characteristics from God. We were made in the image and likeness of God. God Himself breathed the breath of life into man's nostrils and he became a living soul. He didn't do that for animals. Couples who try to push their loved ones to do something they are not called to do are potentially shortening the life span of the very one they love. They are also setting themselves up for relationship problems and possible failure. Always remember this; every relationship you are involved in is either drawing you closer to God or pushing you further away from Him. Being pushed into something that's wrong for you, even with good intentions to push you toward God, can backfire on you and cause a tear in your fellowship with God. God won't change and view you any different, but you can change and view Him differently.

There are times when God will use others such as pastors, mentors, teachers, and some cases spouses to help propel you into your destiny. At that time, you may feel inadequate, unqualified, and fearful. You may or may not see what they see and believe what they believe. Your job in this situation is to go to God and ask for His wisdom and guidance and be open to do whatever He tells you to do. As a pastor I will share with you what I've shared with those in our congregation who feel they have consulted with God, but still are not sure what to do. This is not going to be deep, yet it's very profound. I tell them as their spiritual leader if they can't or don't hear God, then they'll simply have to hear and trust me. Paul said in *1 Corinthians 11:1 "Be ye followers of me, even as I also am of Christ."*

The question that is often asked is, what to do if nothing is happening, I am giving my all, and it feels like I'm beating a dead horse? Stop beating the horse, he's dead already! I encourage you to fast and pray, asking God to reveal His will in this situation. If you see little to no fruit after a prolonged period of time, go back to God and find out if you are doing what He's purposed you to do. I'm not asking you to compare yourself or ministry to others because sometimes you are just out of season, but if you are laboring excessively and fruit is not being produced, then I encourage you to seek wisdom and answers from God on whether or not you are functioning in your call.

There's an old saying, "You cannot put a square peg in a round hole." But I say, "You cannot put a square PIG in a round MOLE. First of all, if you see a square pig and a round mole take pictures, capture them and put them somewhere safe, then get security to watch both you and them because you are about to become very wealthy. A square pig and a round mole, wow, unheard of.

PLEASE, DO US ALL A FAVOR AND DON'T TRY TO PUT PEOPLE IN SHOES THAT DON'T FIT THEM!

Your feet are in constant pain. As long as your shoes are on, you have pain whether you move or remain still.

This means you are in constant pain regardless of what's happening around you. Pain when things go bad and pain when they go well. If you've been elevated to a position and it seems there is no escape from pain, you may be in the wrong position. This pain could be mental, physical, emotional, or financial. The requirements and day-to-day task of the position may be too much for you. Remember, you didn't ask for these shoes, someone put them on your feet for you.

Never allow anyone or any position to cause you constant pain without you making some adjustments. Life is more than pleasing people and holding a position that you are not ready, called, or qualified for. You will be better suited for something else. Stepping down does not make you a failure, but it could keep you alive. I am not authorizing you to become a quitter as soon as you experience opposition or pain. What I am saying is that if all you ever accomplish is pain in your position, you can accomplish the same without the position. We are not what we do. We do because of who we are.

I believe most people in the world have gotten softer from generation to generation. We no longer want to work for what we get and if it gets hard, we are quick to quit and move on to the next so-called greatest thing. Please excuse my French, German and Ebonics, but I ain't wit dat foolishness at all! If God called you to do something, He will give you the sustaining power to stick with it until it is complete. If you are going to quit anything, quit those things you want to do and stick with what God wants you to do. Remember, we are not what we do. We do because of who we are.

If you have become what you do, you have lost your true identity. Anytime you lose who you are for what you do, your value or self-worth diminishes. Though you may have more, you have become less. Eventually what you have become takes over what you have. Let me illustrate; a man becomes financially wealthy and loses his identity in his wealth. In others words, he's only known for his wealth, but not the person God made him to be. He has more, but he has become less because his value to society has diminished. Eventually his diminished value or self-worth will overtake his wealth and put him in jeopardy of losing it all. You can have them both, the wealth and your self-worth if when the wealth comes you keep your true identity in Christ.

Everyone will not be an effective leader. Leaders are those who accept a challenge and are willing and capable to handle it emotionally, mentally, physically, and financially.

I love what Dr. John Maxwell says in his book *Leadership Gold*, "Don't send your Ducks to Eagle School. If you send your Ducks to Eagle School, you will frustrate the Ducks. If you send your Ducks to Eagle School, you will frustrate the Eagles and if you send your Ducks to Eagle School, you will frustrate yourself."

Everybody won't be an eagle. We must send our Ducks to Duck School so they can get a PHD in Duckology and become the best Duck they can be. Our goal should not be to turn a Duck into an Eagle, but to help the Duck reach the highest potential a Duck can reach.

CHAPTER 3

WANNA BE'S KRYPTONITE: ATTITUDE

I would venture to say one of the main reasons why Wanna Be's never become what they desire to become is because of their attitude.

Your attitude determines your level of success.

A Fortune 500 study found the over ninety percent of the executives they surveyed believed their attitude contributed to their level of success more than anything else. When you have a positive attitude, you address negative circumstances with the belief that things will either change for the better or they will have little to no effect on you and your endeavors.

If you are looking to train someone for a leadership position, a positive attitude should be one of the top characteristics the person possesses. If you are training someone with a bad or negative attitude, you must first understand that both of you are at an immediate disadvantage. Your level of success will be delayed, and you will see little to no fruit until they make an attitude adjustment. I refuse to spend a great deal of time with people who have bad attitudes. They will not only frustrate you, but also hinder your ability and desire to help others with positive attitudes. What essentially happens is those who deserve and desire your help will not get the best of you but will end up with the rest of you. Every person who is or will be a great leader must decide what level of success he or she desires. That decision begins with their attitude. Make a quality decision today, to work on your attitude and not allow it to become your kryptonite.

Your attitude determines who will be willing to work with you.

If you desire the best to work with you, then you must prove it by having the best attitude. The best gets the best and the rest gets the rest. Those with the best attitudes attract those who are the best.

Often, we don't realize that most people with wisdom, power, resources and authority choose who they want to work with and with all due respect, they have a right to. Because of who they are and their level of success, they decide who they will spend their time helping or mentoring. Just because you know someone well, never take for granted that they are willing to spend time, effort and resources working with you, especially if your attitude stinks. Nobody enjoys working with a person who has a bad or negative attitude. Some are willing to sacrifice and endure the pain, the drain, and the frustration of working with someone with a bad attitude, but most leaders aren't in a hurry to take on that responsibility.

You desire and deserve the best, so make sure you have a positive and excellent attitude. God has thousands of great leaders ready to pour their life into you and others alike but remember many of them get to choose who that will be. Why not you? You are just as deserving as any. Help the best choose to work with you, to help make you the best.

Your attitude is a door opener when you are not qualified to enter that door.
Revelation 3:8

I know thy works: behold, I have set before thee an open door, and no man can shut it: for thou hast a little strength, and hast kept my word, and hast not denied my name.

Most Christians call it favor, and by definition that's exactly what it is, but there are times when your attitude helps create favor. Your attitude can cause doors to open for you even if you don't have a clue about what's going on behind those doors. You may lack experience, education, and knowledge but your positive, pleasant and excellent attitude can get you the job, promotion, position or advancement that you desire. Just the fact that people like being in your presence can open doors that you are not qualified to enter. Over the years I've come to realize that I enjoy being around pleasant people with positive attitudes more than being in the presence of those who have a lot to offer me, yet they have terrible attitudes. God has always opened doors for me even though I was unqualified to walk through those doors. I believe one of the reasons is because I constantly work on having an excellent attitude. There are a ton of areas where others may be superior to me, but I guarantee you, attitude is not one of them. My education level and social economic status may not be able to compete with those who are more qualified than me, but my attitude will open doors that they may never have the opportunity to enter. Please don't misunderstand me. I am not making lite of education because I'm a firm believer in education. But education alone may not be enough to get you where you desire to be. I know many people who are head over hills in debt from obtaining a college degree that they never used and wish they could go through doors that God has opened for me. Our church constantly encourages and has supported those who decided to pursue a higher level of education. But they have all heard me say that education alone is not the answer. You still need God as well as help from others and your great attitude will get you help from both.

Proverbs 16:7 When a man's ways please the LORD, he maketh even his enemies to be at peace with him.

This scripture makes it plain that when our ways are pleasing to the Lord, those who dislike, oppose, and sometimes flat out hate us, will be at peace with us. I promise you, education, popularity, and money can't do that!

To be pleasing to the Lord, we must put our faith in Him as well as love Him and love people. This is the key to having a pleasant, positive and excellent attitude. By following this blueprint, you will begin to see doors open for you that you never imagined would open. You will begin to experience things that was once reserved for those in high places and closed to those who were unqualified. **Your attitude makes the unqualified, qualified!**

Now let's get back to favor.

Your attitude creates both favor and friction.
You can have it your way!
Proverbs 11:27

He that diligently seeketh good procureth favour: but he that seeketh mischief, it shall come unto him.

For nearly 40 years Burger King's slogan was "Have it your way". Several years ago, the company decided to change to a new slogan, but I believe "Have it your way" works well for this section of the book. Your attitude will allow you to have it your way, favor or friction. You get to choose which one you desire. A good, positive and pleasant attitude can create favor and a bad, negative, stinking attitude can create friction.

We all have been in a situation when someone or maybe you silently sprayed the room with the foul odor of gas from the Exit Only Gas Station. The smell permeated the room and everyone there denied it was them who released the gas. The truth of the matter is it didn't matter who did it, you just wanted out until things cleared up. This is exactly how people feel about you when your attitude is stinking and foul. They don't care who you are, they just want out. If they are forced to be around the foul smell of your stinking attitude, they detest it and it eventually creates friction. By the way, everyone likes the clean fresh air of a good, positive and pleasant attitude. A good, positive and pleasant attitude is like a breath of fresh air especially after being in the midst of foul-smelling pollution.

If you desire to walk in favor, adjust your attitude. Favor is waiting on you to show up so it can surround you like a shield.

Those who have received Jesus as Lord and savior already walk in favor with God, but our attitudes help us obtain more favor with man.

Proverbs 3:4

So shalt thou find favour and good understanding in the sight of God and man.

Luke 2:52

And Jesus increased in wisdom and stature, and in favour with God and man.

Even Jesus increased in favor with man. I'm pretty sure He had a great attitude, which caused men to open doors of favor for Him. I don't know about you, but I believe whatever Jesus has is mine and whatever He increased in, I want the same increase. If the greatest and only perfect leader of all times increased in favor with God and man, sign me up.

Favor or friction you choose. The scriptures says in **Deuteronomy 30:19, "I call heaven and earth to record this day against you, that I have set before you life and death, blessing and cursing: therefore choose life, that both thou and thy seed may live:"** It works the same for favor or friction. Choose favor so that both you and your seed may live.

Did you know that favor causes people to solve problems for you? Somebody somewhere is waiting on you to solve your most pressing problem. When you arrive, show them your pleasant, pleasing and excellent attitude so they can release the favor you need. God has already spoken to the heart of man to show you favor, make it easy for them to obey Him.

Your excellent attitude towards God creates favor.

Luke 23:32-43

And there were also two other, malefactors, led with him to be put to death. 33 And when they were come to the place, which is called Calvary, there they crucified him, and the malefactors, one on the right hand, and the other on the left. 34 Then said Jesus, Father, forgive them; for they know not what they do. And they parted his raiment, and cast lots. 35 And the people stood beholding. And the rulers also with them derided him, saying, He saved others; let him save himself, if he be Christ, the chosen of God. 36 And the soldiers also mocked him, coming to him, and offering him vinegar, 37 And saying, If thou be the king of the Jews, save thyself. 38 And a superscription also was written over him in letters of Greek, and Latin, and Hebrew, THIS IS THE KING OF THE

JEWS. 39 And one of the malefactors which were hanged railed on him, saying, If thou be Christ, save thyself and us. 40 But the other answering rebuked him, saying, Dost not thou fear God, seeing thou art in the same condemnation? 41 And we indeed justly; for we receive the due reward of our deeds: but this man hath done nothing amiss. 42 And he said unto Jesus, Lord, remember me when thou comest into thy kingdom. 43 And Jesus said unto him, Verily I say unto thee, To day shalt thou be with me in paradise.

As Jesus hung on the cross there were two more men hanging as well, one on each side of Him. One of the men had a negative, defaming attitude towards Jesus, but the other had the attitude towards Jesus that we all should have. He had an attitude of gratitude, honor and respect. This excellent attitude towards Jesus unlocked the windows of heaven for him when he died. He died with the favor of God upon him. We too can experience the windows of heaven, but ours come in the form of favor while alive. Our attitude towards God creates unlimited favor. God has already given us all things that pertain unto life and godliness. So, we aren't asking or waiting on God to release this favor for us, He already has. But our heart and attitude towards Him causes us to be more open to receive it. To the degree that our hearts are turned towards God is the degree that we will receive everything that He has in store for us. It's important to understand when I say your attitude creates favor; I am not saying that what we do gets God to move on our behalf because He has already moved. I want you to grasp that we are responsible for the amount or degree of receiving from God. The better my attitude towards God and the things of God, the more I receive, not the more He releases. Jesus said I am come that you might have life and have it more abundantly. Since He's come and now resides in the believer, that abundant life is inside of us. We have the task of releasing it from our spirit into manifestation. Having the right attitude towards God and the things of God releases the flow of favor in your life. If the favor is not flowing, then check your heart and attitude toward the kingdom of God. If you want the full flow of favor then release your faith with the proper attitude towards God and people then watch your life overflow with the favor of God.

Your attitude determines who gives themselves to you.

Your attitude determines whether others feel they can trust you or not.

Your attitude determines your level of growth.

Your attitude can determine the longevity of successful relationships.

Your attitude can destroy a God ordained relationship before it begins.

Your attitude determines how you view those you are assigned to help.

Your attitude determines how you are viewed by those who are assigned to help you.

Your attitude determines how high you rise or how low you fall.

Your attitude unlocks your freedom but will also keep you locked into bondage.

Your attitude opens the ears of listeners but closes those same ears.

CHAPTER 4

AS A LEADER, THERE ARE TIMES WHEN YOU ARE THE HUNTER AND TIMES WHEN YOU ARE THE HUNTED

Have you ever been scanning through your television channels and stopped on the Animal Channel? If you have, I'm sure you've seen a lion in strong pursuit of a deer that's running for his life. The deer was enjoying the day, minding his own business, and strolling through the forest munching on some plants, fruit, or grass. Just as the deer gets comfortable in its surroundings, he notices a lion that appears to have something on his mind that's not so pleasant. The lion has locked in on the deer with that death stare that only lions can give and has begun to inch closer and closer towards the deer. The deer now realizes that the lion is not watching it for entertainment but is watching and approaching it for lunch. The deer's life preservation skills kicks in and it comes to grip with the fact that the lion sees it as food and must make the necessary adjustments and do everything in its power to escape the hungry, bloodthirsty lion. Escaping is the only option because any attempt to fight would make it an easy meal for the lion. The decision has been made and the deer immediately takes off running with everything that's in it knowing that one wrong move and life could be over. Without ever looking back, the deer understands that the mean and hungry beast is in full pursuit with all bad intentions. The deer, unlike many leaders, is aware that looking back impedes its forward progress. The deer is fully convinced that looking back doesn't slow the lion down, but conversely allows it to gain ground. What does a lion chasing a deer have to do with leadership? Everything!

Like the deer, there's no need for a leader to focus on the rearview mirror because all his attention should be on the windshield, looking forward. Looking back only impedes the leader's progress. We all have been faced with situations that caused us to think about what we should or could have done or said. That's normal and healthy, but remaining in that state is not. Remaining in that state makes you easy prey for the lions of this world. If you want to slow down or stop, keeping focusing on what should have been.

Sometimes You're the Deer and Sometimes You're the Lion

All great leaders understand that there are times when they are the hunter and are in full pursuit of God's vision for their lives and organization and at the same time they can be the hunted. The enemy will use people to pursue them and their vision like the hungry lion that's hunting a deer.

As a leader, your heart's desire is to fulfill the vision that God has given you, only to find out that everyone, even those close to you, don't share the same desire. There are some people who will pursue the death of you and your vision more ferociously than that of a lion. See, the lion can only run for so long before getting exhausted and eventually giving up on the chase. The people the enemy uses to come after you appear to never get exhausted, but gain energy and enthusiasm as they plot, plan, pursue, and attack like the lion with bad intentions. They are hungry and appear to be bloodthirsty. Nothing and no one are off limits.

This chapter is not designed for you to entertain fear, but it is designed to open your eyes, so you won't be naïve. Just know this: if you're born again, you've already won the battle through Jesus' life, death, and resurrection. But victory does not mean you are void of challenges and that life is easy and everything will be all lovey-dovey. There's an enemy out there who doesn't like you or your assignment and he's not going to sit back and allow you to succeed without putting up a fight. Often the enemy will use those closest to you because he knows they have more influence and insight into your financial, spiritual, and personal affairs. He's also aware that your heart is attached to them, so you will more likely to listen to them than you would anyone else. He understands that your desire to keep peace with them may be stronger than your desire to follow God. This is where the dilemma comes. Are you going to disobey God just to maintain a relationship that is being influenced by Satan? I know your answer, but pay close attention to your actions when it pertains to your loved ones and friends. Sometimes we are not fully aware that our actions are leading us away from God. Holy Spirit may instruct us, but we must be in tune with Him or we will do the very thing we are trying to avoid.

You as the Lion

I recently watched a video of a hunter's deer decoy (a fake deer for those wondering) being attacked by a mountain lion. The mountain lion assumed the deer decoy was real and went in for the kill only to find out it wasn't the real thing. Likewise, sometimes the wrong person is attacked in the enemy's pursuit of the leader and sometimes the leader attacks the wrong person in pursuit of their enemy.

The pastor's family is a prime target for attacks that weren't meant for them. They just happen to be the closest to him. Some attackers are simply spineless and instead of going to the source, they work their way to his family in order to make their displeasure known. As a pastor, I have made it known to my congregation that my family is off limits. Any issues, questions, or misunderstandings about my decisions or me should come directly to me. If you want me to become the lion, then go after my family. For those of you who are familiar with me, you know that I am an easy-going, fun-loving guy. Well, most of the time. (That's my story and I'm sticking with it.) But I don't take lightly attacks on my underserving family when I am the one you want. Never make the mistake of going after the innocent in order to affect the one you deem guilty.

Correction can Lead to Rejection

Leaders should always use wisdom in how they correct and criticize. This may not sound biblical, but everybody should not be treated the same.

Hear me out before you close the book. Everyone can't handle the same type of correction or criticism. After being corrected, some go into rejection mode. They reject everything the leader says and attempt to do. They reject further correction and they reject the leader's sincere heart felt desire to help them improve. When dealing with this person, you must have compassion and understand that there's a root cause of this issue and you are not it. Most people who have a rejection issue brought that with them to your organization. Some felt rejected as a child and never dealt with it properly, therefore they have rejection issues as an adult. Others may have been abandoned and are without love, help, or direction. There are many reasons why one may feel rejected when being corrected. Below is a short list of reasons people feel rejected:

Abandonment

Dysfunctional Family

Verbal Abuse

Domestic Violence

Bullying

Pride

Comparison

Legalism

Death of a loved one

This list can go on and on. We don't necessarily have to know what triggered the rejection, but we need to know how to help them feel loved and accepted if they allow it. Many who feel rejected by you will cut you off permanently. They will have nothing to do with you and if you are somewhere they were planning to go, they won't go because you are there. They will miss meaningful appointments, God ordained assignments, their children's school, and recreational events just to avoid being in your presence. Some have lost employment and refused higher paying positions or promotions to avoid you. I know this may sound foolish to you, but it's real to them.

Straight from the Hip or the Sandwich Principle?

There are some people who need you to just shoot straight from the hip and others need the sandwich principle in order to keep them from being offended. The sandwich principle is when you are correcting someone; you give him or her the bread, then the meat or what you really wanted to say in the beginning, followed by more bread. In other words, you encourage and compliment them on the person they are, what they excel at or how well they are doing in an area, then you correct their actions, followed by more encouragement. You always want them to leave thinking about how they can improve and not about how rude you were to them or how bad you treated them.

Leaders should not mistreat people just because they have the power and authority to do so. You don't have to be rude or condescending in order to get your point across. Remember you are the one in charge, so you get to make the decisions. Make your decision and then deal with people accordingly. You can be firm without being rude. Being rude is not a characteristic that authorities look for when they are evaluating you for a promotion.

Philippians 2:3

Let nothing be done through strife or vainglory; but in lowliness of mind let each esteem other better than themselves.

If you've ever noticed, lions don't make a lot of noise when they attack. Why? Because they already know they are in charge and their decision has been made, now you must deal with it. They are going to do whatever they are going to do. They don't need an introduction or fanfare. They feel as if they are the kings of the jungle and it all belongs to them. Therefore, they feel no need to warn you that you are their next meal. Besides, noise might run you away.

As a leader we must mimic the lion by making sound decisions without making a sound. We don't have to let everyone know that we are coming to deal with someone or another individual. Only the appropriate people and the individual should be aware that you are planning to handle business.

Contrary to lions, we as leaders don't attack to do harm or kill, but we attack for the benefit of both the person and the organization. Our attack is meant to correct, with the intent to build up, reinforce, strengthen, and to improve both the person and the organization. This is a win-win situation. We win because the organization improves and they win because they improve. Unfortunately, all attacks don't end this way. Some people are not receptive to correction and damage themselves more as well as the organization. You win some and I don't like to say it, but you lose some. But it's not our job to determine whether they will be receptive or not. Our job is to correct in love with the intention of leaving with the win-win outcome. It's sad, but there are times when you will be the only winner. If a person is not receptive to correction and decide they no longer want to be a part of your organization, in this situation, you're the only winner. Please don't misunderstand what I'm saying here. If someone's attitude is closed to correction, they are damaging others and your organization whether you know it or not. Bless them with your words or gifts and release them. You pray that they have a heart change and hope they get the necessary help and become all God intended for them to be. Then you move on and clean up any mess they left behind and love the people they left behind. If you as a leader have done your job correctly, you already have someone trained and skilled to step in, so nothing goes lacking. The person who left may be missed, but the organization should continue to move forward.

I've talked to several people who have left churches and act like they were so special that the church would most certainly miss them because they were this or that. They go on and on like the church is in trouble now that they are gone. Until I asked them this one question: "How many churches have closed since you left?" A few answered none, but most refused to answer at all. When leaders do their jobs correctly, nothing and no one should impede the progress of the organization because another leaves.

As lion-like leaders we should attack every area we are assigned to with the mindset and attitude that we will be successful in our endeavors. Then strategically plan and implement systems that lead us towards that success.

CHAPTER 5

DON'T BE LIKE THE FLATTENED SQUIRREL LYING IN THE ROAD

I find it amazing how squirrels safely run back and forth from one side of the road to the other. Very seldom do you see one who didn't make it safely to the other side. While driving to the office one day, I realized why one dead squirrel didn't make it to the other side safely. He kept changing his mind, which way he should go. It all boils down to decisions. Like the squirrels, sometimes we are in a battle of choices. We have so many options until we struggle with what is the correct decision to make. Mimicking the squirrel, we go back and forth and keep changing our minds about which way to go. Sad to say, often we are flattened by our circumstances and end up like the squirrels that couldn't decide which way to go. We may start off right, but then turn around only to find that the way we were going was the correct way. That's why it is vitally important that leaders have a solid relationship with God.

James 1:5

If any of you lack wisdom, let him ask of God, that giveth to all men liberally, and upbraideth not; and it shall be given him.

Rebellion verses Witchcraft

Our first step to making good, sound decisions is to go to God first and ask what we should do. Anything other than this can and will lead to disaster. God says He will give us wisdom if we simply ask Him for it.

Sometimes we don't ask God for help because we already know what we need to do but just won't do it. If this is you, then ask Him to help you with rebellion. According to the Oxford Dictionary, rebellion is an act of violent or open resistance to an established government or ruler; the action or process of resisting authority, control, or convention. When we don't do what we know we are supposed to do, we are deciding to rebel against God.

1 Samuel 15:23

For rebellion is as the sin of witchcraft, and stubbornness is as iniquity and idolatry. Because thou hast rejected the word of the LORD, he hath also rejected thee from being king.

According to this scripture, God sees rebellion the same as He sees witchcraft. Now, most believers would be very offended if you told them they're rebellion is seen as witchcraft. But it's in the Bible. When we rebel against God and authority, our decisions are rooted in rebellion. Therefore, any major decision we make, automatically begins from a negative, sinful place in our minds and heart. This is one reason why some people seem to go from one bad decision to another and it appears to be a never-ending cycle. Our decisions come from what we think or how we feel. So, if our minds and hearts are diseased with rebellion, then our decisions and actions will reflect it.

The lifestyle of rebellious people attracts others with the same attitude. This is how cliques are formed. One rebellious person connects with another, then another, and another. It won't take long before there's a room full of rebellious believers who think they are doing the will of God.

How Does Rebellion Express itself?

Rebellion expresses itself through the personalities of people. You can quickly pick up on it when you hear, well that's just the way I am. I'm not changing just because I'm in the presence of the pastor or the boss. Well, I'm just outspoken and I don't have to bite my tongue for no one. He's a man just like me; it's not like he's God or something. I've got to be real with you. You guys are so fake acting like this man is something special.

He put his pants on just like me. This is usually rebellion speaking, expressing itself through their personality.

Rebellion also expresses itself through those who hunger and thirst for a position of leadership or control. These people only want the position of power in order to promote their own personal ideas and agenda, not the agenda of God or their leader. They will subtly buck against anything the leader attempts to do so that it will not prosper. After the leader's failed attempt, they will promote their ideas and agenda with the expectation of the leader's full cooperation, acknowledgement, and financial support. These people want to be publicly recognized in an attempt to draw others into their web of lies and deceit. If these people are in a position of leadership, there will be a lack of unity, trust, love, and teamwork in the organization. A leader should not have a heart to build his own kingdom, but a heart to serve.

Rebellion expresses itself through those who are jealous of those in authority. Merriam Webster Dictionary defines jealous as being hostile toward a rival or one believed to enjoy an advantage.

Rebellion shows up when one believes that their leader has an advantage over them. Often those that are rebelling against authority do so because the leader is the decision maker and because others do what he asks of them. They desire to do or be what the leader is, but don't want to do what the leader has done to get to where he is. Therefore, they rebel because they are not in the leader's position, but feel they are equal to or greater than the leader. They also think the leader has no idea about how they feel about him. So, they smile in their presence and try to be as cordial as possible, while they are in turmoil internally as they watch the leader prosper and advance. Make no mistake about it; we leaders know those who are jealous of us. Holy Spirit may not give you the exact words of jealousy, but He informs you that they are not for you and their heart is not knitted to you. He tells you that they have driven a wedge between you and themselves and until their heart changes, the relationship in irreparable. In this situation trying to force a relationship with them could actually make the relationship worse. Love them, pray for them, treat them as others with dignity and respect, but do not waste your life and precious time trying to fix something that the other party wants broken. You can only make this work when the other party is willing to see, repent, and move forward. This does not make them a terrible person; it makes them a person who needs a heart change and you are who God uses to help change hearts. The love, respect, and care you show the person despite how they feel about you is a powerful tool to help them see the love of God and see their need for repentance. Love doesn't mean wasting countless hours trying to get them to like, understand, and change towards you. Love means you treat them like Jesus treated those who were against Him. He told them the truth, gave them the solution and helped them when they needed Him. There is no love without truth. If you have contributed to the way this person feels about you, repent, ask for their forgiveness, and be careful to never make the same mistake that contributed to their actions. But always remember to never take the blame for something that's out of your control. You cannot be the blame for others rebellion. Rebellion is a heart and mind issue and if that heart and mind doesn't belong to you, you are not the blame.

As a leader you are equipped to handle and help to restore those who are rebellious if they desire restoration. God has gifted you with everything you need to deal with rebellion. Leaders are anointed to minister to all kinds of people and there are those who won't make it easy. There are some people who are not sent by the enemy, even though they may act like it at times. They are without understanding, need to be taught, connected to the wrong people, immature, and some hurt. There are many other reasons why people act the way they do, but a good leader has the tools to correct, enhance, and help advance them.

Rebellion can also express itself through those who have a higher level of education than their leader, those who are financially secure, those who have a strong reputation in the community, and those who are spiritually gifted. This rebellion comes in the form of pride. I know from experience that none of us claim to have it, but all of us can see it in everyone who does.

Proverb 16:18

Pride goeth before destruction, and an haughty spirit before a fall.

Proverbs 29:23

A man's pride shall bring him low: but honour shall uphold the humble in spirit.

As you travel and run across a flattened squirrel lying in the road, let it be a reminder to you that this is what happens when you don't make the right decision in time.

He struggled with his decision-making process.

He started out right, but turned around

CHAPTER 6

DON'T PLAY WITH SNAKES, THEY CAN BE DEADLY

Don't you just love it when you see people handling snakes and someone questions their action and they give them the famous supposed to be comforting line, "Oh, it won't harm you, this kind is not poisonous." I don't know about you, but that brings me no comfort at all. It's still a snake and the way I see it, all snakes can be deadly whether they are poisonous or not. Some snakes are amazingly strong. I watched a snake on the internet wrap around a man's neck and cut off his air supply then squeezed the very life out of him. That's probably rare, but it has happened on more than one occasion.

The reason I say don't play with snakes is because some can choke you, some are poisonous, and they all bite. Being that I don't have time to figure out which one does what, wisdom says don't play with any of them.

Sometimes people can act like snakes, they choke the life out of you, some are poisonous, and they all bite. I've seen many naive leaders get choked, bitten, and poisoned by snakes in their organization. In most organizations, there are only a few snakes that hang around long enough to do damage. But the damage they do can be devastating.

When snakes in your organization choke, they draw all the life out of whomever they get attached to. They play with you, tell jokes, help with a need, pray with you, do whatever is necessary to get close to you, and then they latch hold of you and choke the life out of you. If you have ever spent time around someone and every time you leave the person you are drained for no apparent reason, you've been choked!

To Be or Not to Be

Snakes don't become snakes by accident. Either they choose to follow that path, or they have been chosen and groomed by a larger more powerful snake. But believe me, it is definitely on purpose. God has given us a free will. We choose whom we are going to follow. We may not have had a choice when we were children, but once we became old enough to make our own decision, we chose our own path. Our environment, life experiences, and people we trust may have influenced us, but we still chose our own path. People choose whether they want to hurt, hinder, or destroy others. What makes it worse is they act as if they are doing the right thing. As a counselor, I have talked with several people who do evil and yet call it good.

Isaiah 5:20

Woe unto them that call evil good, and good evil; that put darkness for light, and light for darkness; that put bitter for sweet, and sweet for bitter!

Just as we Choose to do Evil, we can also Choose to do Good

Deuteronomy 30:15

See, I have set before thee this day life and good, and death and evil;

Deuteronomy 30:19

I call heaven and earth to record this day against you, that I have set before you life and death, blessing and cursing: therefore choose life, that both thou and thy seed may live:

The leader, who chooses life and blessings, also chooses life and blessings for his followers. As leaders, our choices have the power to affect many generations to come whether be it positive or negative. Because of our position and influence we can be very instrumental in changing the lives of those we lead. I admonish you not to take this lightly. Your role as a leader is far more than just a title or position. Your role is an example that will be followed and emulated. What you do and how you do it will be placed under a magnifying glass and will be complemented and followed by some but criticized and rejected by others. Let the people make their choice, but you make the choice to do what you do to the best of your ability and trust God to add His super on your natural.

We are forced to make decisions every day. Some are difficult and others are easy. Our decisions are like roads, some are smooth, bumpy, long, short, and some rocky. Regardless of the type of road you are on, there's one thing they have in common, they all are leading you somewhere. It may lead to a place you didn't desire to go but ended up there. Like roads, every decision we make is leading us somewhere. We may not like where they take us, but the outcome was based on a decision we made. Some of our decisions are smooth and short, we don't have to think about them much or get any advice. They just flow right along with life. Others are long, bumpy, rough and uncomfortable. You feel these decisions as you are making them. You experience pain and discomfort as you make the decision, knowing the outcome may be just as bad or worse than the decision-making process itself. These are the decisions that determine your level of success. Most of the time, it's not the easy, smooth decisions that determine your success. If it were, everyone would be successful in every endeavor. It's when you are faced with the long, hard, rocky, rough, and uncomfortable decision that you pass the test of leadership. Making the right decision when it's hard is what makes you a powerful, successful leader. Great leaders make decisions that could cost them their existence in the organization or even their lives. The decisions that cost you the most, usually gives you the greatest return. The more challenging the decision, the more gratifying the reward. In leadership, the decision you fear the most may be the one that rewards you the best.

Eight things to remember when a decision must be made:

1. Pray before you make the decision and ask for wisdom.
2. When you make the decision, make it based on Godly principles.
3. Get understanding about whatever you are dealing with.
4. Make sure your priorities are in order and your heart is right

before making the decision.

5. Believe God for the desired results.

6. Make up your mind that you can handle the outcome.

7. If you begin to see things that appear contrary to your desired results, don't cave in and give up. Speak the desired results and thank God as if your desired results have already manifested.

8. Walk by faith and not by fear.

Don't ever make a decision that needs God's attention without consulting Him first. It's not wise to make the decision and then pray and ask God to bless it. By doing this, you could be asking God to bless a decision that He didn't want you to make. If God didn't want you to make the decision you made, why would He bless it? Wise leaders ask God first, and then proceed with His desires.

James 1:5

If any of you lack wisdom, let him ask of God, that giveth to all men liberally, and upbraideth not; and it shall be given him.

All decisions should be based upon Godly principles. If your decisions are based on Godly principles, your outcome will resemble Godly results. I don't want to give you the impression that just because your decision is based on Godly principles that they will always generate the results you desire. They may not produce your desired results, but more times than not, they will resemble Godly results. In other words, even when you don't get the results you desired, you may still have peace that everything will work together for your good. Also, what you desired may not have been God's best for you; therefore, He made adjustments for you so things would work out better and in your favor. Sometimes when things don't turn out the way we desire them to, we get discouraged and forget to ask God for His assistance. Other times we may need to wait on God and have some patience. Godly results can take more time than fleshly results when others are involved. For some things to work out, the heart of several people may need to change. Unfortunately, we don't know how many people need a change of heart, how many people have a part to play in the decision, and who those people are. We may not have these answers, neither do we need to know them because the heart of the king is in the hand of God and He turns it whichever way He wills.

Proverbs 21:1

The king's heart is in the hand of the LORD, as the rivers of water: he turneth it whithersoever he will.

Before we make any decision, we must first get understanding about the situation. It's not wise to make blind decisions. Blind decisions are decisions we make in the blind or without knowledge of what's really going on. If you are like me, you've made these before, especially when it comes to one of our loved ones. Boy can they get you! They only tell you what they want you to know, and then ask for you to intervene. After hearing their plea, you jump headfirst only to discover there was more to the story. Too late, their mess has become yours. I've seen it where once someone jumps into their loved one's mess, the loved one jumps out and leave them in the fire to be burned. I have been on both ends of the spectrum. I've been the loved one and the blind decision maker. In both scenarios, I realized I made a bad decision and wished I could change the negative outcome. Unfortunately, in life, there are times when we won't get a do over, that's why it is vitally important to get understanding before making decisions.

Make sure your priorities are in order and your heart is right before making a decision. One may ask why is this so important? It's important because decisions made with improper priorities causes improper results. If your priorities are out of order, your decisions could produce something you are not ready for, shouldn't have, or not qualified to handle yet.

Genesis 16:1-5

1 Now Sarai Abram's wife bare him no children: and she had an handmaid, an Egyptian, whose name was Hagar. 2 And Sarai said unto Abram, Behold now, the LORD hath restrained me from bearing: I pray thee, go in unto my maid; it may be that I may obtain children by her. And Abram hearkened to the voice of Sarai. 3 And Sarai Abram's wife took

Hagar her maid the Egyptian, after Abram had dwelt ten years in the land of Canaan, and gave her to her husband Abram to be his wife. 4 And he went in unto Hagar, and she conceived: and when she saw that she had conceived, her mistress was despised in her eyes. 5 And Sarai said unto Abram, My wrong be upon thee: I have given my maid into thy bosom; and when she saw that she had conceived, I was despised in her eyes: the LORD judge between me and thee.

Abram and Sarai priorities were not in order and they decided they would take things in their own hands and not wait on God. When Sarai realized that their decision was not the right one, it was too late. Now she must deal with this decision the rest of their lives. What she thought she was ready for, she wasn't. It wasn't her time or season for what she desired. Like Sarai, we too can make rash decision with improper priorities and end up in a state of regret. I don't know anyone who enjoys living their life regretting decisions they've made from improper priorities. If you desire to lead successfully, you must only make decisions when your priorities are in order and your heart is right before God and people.

Never make a major decision without believing God for the desired results. What good is it to make a decision about what you desire if you are not willing to believe God it will come to pass? There will be times when you are not the decision maker, but the decision will affect you, so you must then believe God for the desired results as if you were the one making the decision. Paul was a prisoner on a ship that was headed for disaster because the captain and the guards refused to take heed to Paul's advice.

Acts 27:21-25

21 But after long abstinence Paul stood forth in the midst of them, and said, Sirs, ye should have hearkened unto me, and not have loosed from Crete, and to have gained this harm and loss. 22 And now I exhort you to be of good cheer: for there shall be no loss of any man's life among you, but of the ship. 23 For there stood by me this night the angel of God, whose I am, and whom I serve, 24 Saying, Fear not, Paul; thou must be brought before Caesar: and, lo, God hath given thee all them that sail with thee. 25 Wherefore, sirs, be of good cheer: for I believe God, that it shall be even as it was told me.

I Believe God, it will be just as He Told me

Even though Paul wasn't the ultimate decision maker, his life was going to be affected by the one who would make the decisions. Paul had a Word from God that they would make it safely through the storm and no one would die. Paul made up his mind that he would believe God for those exact results. He didn't waver or lose heart when faced with trouble and danger, he held on to that Word and simply believed God. How did he do it?

Acts 19:21 says Paul had already purposed in his spirit to go to Rome. Then in Acts 23:11 the Lord had spoken to him that he would testify of Jesus in Rome. So Paul was destined to make it, but the other men on the ship didn't have the relationship with the Lord like Paul. Therefore, it was no guarantee they would make it until the Angel spoke to Paul. It's a strong possibility they all would have died if Paul had not been on the ship with them.

Acts 27:24

Saying, Fear not, Paul; thou must be brought before Caesar: and, lo, God hath given thee all them that sail with thee.

Notice God said He had given **Paul** all those who were sailing with him. This proves that there may be times when some people will not get where they are supposed to be unless they stay connected to your leadership. If they leave you prematurely, it could be detrimental to their destiny and even their lives. After leaving, some may appear to be prospering in some areas of life, but that may be short lived and it won't be the area God has designed for them. This shouldn't cause you to get puffed up in pride, but it should cause you to take seriously your leadership position and recognize that God has entrusted people into your care to get them where He desires them to be. I know this is easier said than done, but we too must be like Paul and believe God in the midst of unfavorable circumstances.

Can you Handle it?

We won't always hear God's voice before we make every decision, but the decision still must be made. Leaders must make some decisions at the spur of the moment. You must settle in your heart that you are able to handle the outcome of your decision before you give the final ok. Some years ago, as I was studying leadership, one of the suggestions that were made was to ask yourself if I do this and it doesn't turn out the way I thought, will I be able to handle the outcome? It was also suggested to ask yourself what's the worst that could happen if I do this? Then if you can live with the worst thing that could happen, you are ready to make the decision. While I don't disagree with those suggestions, I like to ask myself, what's the best thing that could happen if I make this decision? The best thing gives you a glimpse or picture of the good results you desire, so that you have something to connect your faith to. It's hard for me to connect my faith if all I'm thinking about is the worst thing that could happen. Surely, we need to know and be prepared for whatever may happen, but that shouldn't be our focus.

Leaders have the ability to remain focused on their desired outcome in spite of what's happening right before their eyes. You can be witnessing the worst, but still envisioning the best. This is a sign that your faith and leadership skills are turbo-charged and ready for action. This is also a sign that you have not allowed circumstances to create doubt and hinder your faith. If you can remain focused on your desired results in the midst of trials and negative circumstances, you have conquered the scheme that the enemy uses to destroy millions of leaders and their vision. Broken focus is one of the main reasons why leaders fail. The enemy tries all he can to get you to lose focus on what's really important. When you lose focus on the most important thing, you can't be trusted to lead effectively. At this point, your decision mechanism is out of whack and problems are inevitable and as a leader, when you have prolonged unsolved problems, you can't lead effectively and eventually you create problems for your followers. Therefore, it's very important that you don't major on the minor. Spending your time worried and thinking on things that are not important causes you to lose focus, time, energy, resources, and your followers. If God called you to lead, then you have the ability to remain focused on the things that matter the most. It may take some effort on your part, but you have it in you and you can do it. I encourage you to set aside time daily to prioritize what's important in your life and what God would have you to focus on. If everything is important, then nothing is important.

If Things Appear Contrary to your Desired Results, Keep Speaking the Word and don't Cave in and Give up

There will be times when you make decisions that may not turn out as planned. These may not be the wrong decision, but the results may be taking longer than expected. This is a time when the enemy and your mind begin to play tricks on you. You begin to see things contrary to what you were believing for. You begin to feel as if the results are alluding you instead of moving towards you. Don't buy the lie! Keep speaking the Word and don't cave into the pressure and give up. Faith never gives up when what it is targeting is the will of God! If it's the will of God for you, know and understand that God has already given it to you and you are just standing, believing, and waiting for the manifestation.

2 Peter 1:3

According as his divine power hath given unto us all things that pertain unto life and godliness, through the knowledge of him that hath called us to glory and virtue:

Regardless of what things may look like, speak the Word and thank God as if it's already manifested and you have it in your possession. According to 2 Peter 1:3 if Jesus died for you to have it, and you are born again, you already have it. It also says we get it through the knowledge that we have of God. Increase your knowledge of God and you will see more manifestation of what Jesus died for you to have. If it pertains to life and godliness, He has already given it to you. Everything that Jesus died for us to have is in our born-again spirit.

John 4:24

"God is a Spirit: and they that worship him must worship him in spirit and in truth."

This means God deals with us through our born-again spirit. So, whatever He has given us is in our born-again spirit. It's our job to bring it forth from the spirit to the natural.

John 6:63

"It is the spirit that quickeneth; the flesh profiteth nothing: the words that I speak unto you, they are spirit, and they are life."

This is Jesus speaking and He said the Words He speaks are spirit and life. So, the way to bring to life what's in our spirit is to speak the Word of God. "Quickeneth" in this verse means to vitalize and to make alive. It is our born-again spirit and the Word of God that makes things come alive in our lives. As we speak the Word of God, it connects and bears witness in our spirit, then the spirit quickens what we speak and makes it come alive and manifest in the natural. Keep speaking the Word and thanking God for the manifestation. Then after you receive the manifestation, continue thanking Him for it being manifested.

Walk by Faith, not by Facts, Foolishness, or Fear

I hear leaders talk about facts as if facts are the final authority. The Word of God is final authority. Facts are simply information that has been proven. But it doesn't mean facts can't be changed. I'm a witness that facts are ever changing. Some years ago, I was experiencing major knee pain. It felt like every time I moved there was a grinding in my knee. After some time of prayer and laying on of hands, I went to the doctor and he took x-rays of my knee. To my surprise the x-rays proved that I had a problem larger than I anticipated. Bone on bone. There was no cartilage between the bones in my knee. Whenever I walked or moved my leg, I could hear the noise of the bones rubbing against each other and that just made the pain more excruciating. My doctor gave me some options to think about, but as he was completing his spill, he said to me, I know you are going home to pray this away. I replied with something like you got that right, because the cartilage is back in my knee now. He gave me a free sample of medication for pain, but we both knew I wasn't going to take it unless I had to. He scheduled me for a return visit to discuss my options. During this visit he explained to me that the cartilage wasn't going to return on its own. During the visit we also decided to take another x-ray because I informed him that his information was too late, the pain was gone, and the cartilage had already returned. This time to his surprise the new x-ray showed cartilage around the bones and we no longer heard the grinding noise. He compared the old x-rays to the new ones and had no other choice but to recognize that only the power of God could do what he was witnessing. We laughed together and then he kicked me out of his office and jokingly told me I was bad for business. Both of us gave God praise for the miracle He'd performed and I never returned with that problem again. I share this story because the x-rays were facts. The information/pictures proved that there was no cartilage between the bones in my knee on my first visit, but God changed the facts. He put cartilage back and took away the pain. We walk by faith, not by facts, foolishness, or fear.

Don't ever be moved by what your senses tell you, instead, walk by faith. Faith is your actions or reactions that causes you to move towards what God has already provided. If you are not moving towards what God has already provided, then you are not walking by faith. Likewise, if you are in fact moving toward what God has not provided through Jesus' death, burial, and resurrection, then you are not walking by faith but by foolishness. Walking by faith in what Jesus has already done on the cross changes the information your senses give you.

CHAPTER 7

YOU WILL BE FOLLOWED OR AVOIDED

Y ou are an example and you will be either followed or avoided. Dictionary.com defines example as a pattern or model, as of **something to be imitated or avoided**. You may be an example to others, but your example could be an example not to be followed.

1 Corinthians 11:1

> *Be ye followers of me, even as I also am of Christ.*

Paul instructed his followers to follow him as he followed Christ. If we follow Paul's example, people should be eager to follow us. If people are avoiding following you, then you should make sure that you are following Christ. The best way to get others to follow you is to first become successful at leading yourself. If you are following Christ the way you should, then others will get on board with you.

Don't be Flaky, Fake, Phony, or Full of Yourself

Not many people I know would follow someone that's flakey. The Merriam-Webster Dictionary defines flakey as not reliable in performance or behavior: Undependable. If you want people to avoid you like the plague, then be unreliable in your performance or behavior. Even worse, be undependable. Anyone who is not reliable in performance or behavior and undependable should not hold a position of leadership. I have made this mistake before when I didn't listen to others who warned me about the performance and behavior of people I was prepping for leadership. I proceeded to give them leadership positions and boy did I have a rude awakening. I found out that some of them were as flaky as corn flakes without the sugar. But to my credit, the people who were telling me that my leaders to be were flaky were indeed flaky themselves and that's why I didn't pay them any attention.

Sometimes the heart sees what is invisible to the eye. - H. Jackson Brown

Even when love isn't enough, somehow it is. - Stephen King

1 Peter 3:8-11

Finally, be ye all of one mind, having compassion one of another, love as brethren, be pitiful, be courteous: 9 Not rendering evil for evil, or railing for railing: but contrariwise blessing; knowing that ye are thereunto called, that ye should inherit a blessing. 10 For he that will love life, and see good days, let him refrain his tongue from evil, and his lips that they speak no guile: 11 Let him eschew evil, and do good; let him seek peace, and ensue it.

Proverbs 4:14-18

Enter not into the path of the wicked, and go not in the way of evil men. 15 Avoid it, pass not by it, turn from it, and pass away. 16 For they sleep not, except they have done mischief; and their sleep is taken away, unless they cause some to fall. 17 For they eat the bread of wickedness, and drink the wine of violence. 18 But the path of the just is as the shining light, that shineth more and more unto the perfect day.

How Much of You do you have in your Tank?

One thing that irritates most people are leaders who are full of themselves. Some people are super-gifted, intelligent, smart, sharp, nice looking, charismatic, and know their job well, but have trouble with leadership because they are too full of themselves. By the way, being full of yourself is not a good thing. Thousands of leaders have failed because they didn't understand this and couldn't get over themselves. Instead of acknowledging their shortcomings, they try to justify how they are by calling it confidence. Please don't mistake being full of yourself for confidence. Being confident in who you are or in your ability does not come close to resembling being full of yourself. Confidence in who you are doesn't look down on others who don't have what you have or perform as well as you do. Confident people don't mind helping those who are not as gifted or knowledgeable as they are. Those who are full of themselves don't want others to do what they do or know what they know because they feel they will lose their competitive edge. Confidence says I can have my desire regardless of what another does or knows. I'm not naive enough to think that everybody needs to know everything you know. There is certain information that leaders are privy to, that followers shouldn't know until they are in leadership. Too much or the wrong information in the hands of the wrong people can be devastating to an organization. At times, leaders who are full of themselves can be worse for an organization than the wrong people with information that they shouldn't have.

Signs you are full of yourself:

You think others love you just as much as you love yourself – When people are full of themselves, they have a false sense or worth. They believe others feel the same way about them as they feel about themselves. This couldn't be further from the truth. When you are full of yourself, you love yourself far more than others will love you. You are always on your mind, but not always on others minds. When you are concerned about what's happening in your life, they are concerned about what's happening in their lives.

You love to promote yourself - If you're the best thing going then how are you going to improve? You promote yourself because you feel like you are the greatest or the best thing going. Therefore, your conversations are usually centered around you. If you falsely believe that you have arrived and you are "**IT**," then you will miss the people that God has ordained you to glean from. Growth and advancement usually comes when we humble ourselves and learn what others know, then add our knowledge and wisdom to it.

You must be seen, heard or noticed - People who are full of themselves believe when they enter a room all attention should be on them. But, if it is not, they will make sure that it is. They thrive for and seek after attention. I mean how can you not see me? Don't you know who I am? This is their mentality. You need to recognize me, give me your undivided attention, and make sure others get the memo as well.

You are always in competition - Competition is not always a bad thing, but it can be if you are full of yourself. If you have to outdo everyone all the time, you have this issue. If you must purchase a nicer car because your neighbor, friend, or sibling's car is newer or more advanced than yours, you are full of yourself and are headed for a terrible, dissatisfied, unsettling life. Competition is ok if you are competing to be the best you that you can be and, in the process, you supersede everyone else. There's nothing wrong with you desiring to be number one. But if you are full of yourself, your biggest desire is to unseat number two regardless of what it takes. When you are full of yourself, you forget about having ethical and moral values. Compete with yourself and be the best you that you can be, then enjoy being number one and on top. Anytime your attention leaves you and becomes focused on the person ahead of you, there will be temptation to do ungodly things to surpass them.

You are too concerned with your looks - I strongly agree that we should look our best or at least desire to look presentable. But if you are obsessed with your good looks, you are full of yourself. I have seen some people who I believe are married to the mirror. They spend more time in the mirror than some spend with the one they married. Tuck your shirt back in, put your hair back in place, add a little skin moisturizer, yea freshen-up some, but don't fall so in love with what you see in the mirror that you become no good to the ones who actually see you.

You feel threatened by others' success - You shouldn't be threatened by others' success. Their success is not an enemy to you. If you are threatened by another's success, it's a possibility that you don't believe you can reach or surpass their level of success. It's also possible that you have some hidden jealousy, insecurities, and feelings of inferiority. While you may never express these feelings, you tell stories in your head like, "They always get what they want and never have to work hard for it." Here's another, "If we switched places, they wouldn't have all of that and they'd be in a worse position than I'm in now and if I put their shoes on, I would have a whole lot more than what they have." Sounds familiar? If so, ask yourself these questions: What is it about their success that has me feeling threatened? What can I learn from them and what they've accomplished that can help me accomplish my desires? Once you honestly answer these questions, celebrate their success, learn what you can from them and their accomplishments, and then place your attention on what you need to do to reach the level of success you desire. Here are several more signs that you are full of yourself:

You love talking about yourself.

You struggle with submission to someone you feel doesn't add up to your standards.

You over promise but under deliver.

You want more and more just to look like you have it going on.

You do and say things to try to get people to compliment you.

Your ego is out of control.

CHAPTER 8

TODAY WILL NEVER HAPPEN AGAIN

Are you aware that you are making history today? Today will never happen again and you are experiencing it. Those who have passed on or are yet to be born will never experience today. You are a part of history, so why not make the best of it?

I love this quote from Dr. Seuss: "Today you are you! That is truer than true! There is no one alive who is you-er than you!" How powerful is that? You should take time to think and meditate on this quote. Today you are you! You are who you are, so be the best you that you can be. After all, no one else is good enough to be you! Every day you wake up, you should celebrate you. If for no other reason than you are the only you in the world; that makes you special. I believe we spend too much time trying to be who we think we should be and trying to be like who we desire to be like. You can never be anyone other than you. We should learn, glean, follow, and serve our mentors and leaders, but never deduce ourselves to trying to be them. By the way, it's a waste of time because you will never be them.

Psalms 118:24

This is the day which the LORD hath made; we will rejoice and be glad in it.

This is the only day that will be this day and you are the only you that is living this day. I know this is sort of a tongue twister, but this statement will change your life when you get revelation about it. Maybe I can help you better understand it. God made today to be today and He made you to be you. So, the way I see it is, God made this day for you and you for today. You are here for a purpose for such a time as this. You are here to live a day that will never be experienced again. God knew you had something special to add to life and history. No longer should you walk around acting as if today is not important. Both you and this day are extremely important and will add value to the lives of others.

Great leaders understand the value of today. Today is the only time you will have to plan, strategize, implement, and impact the world in which you live. I know my faith-based readers are saying, the devil is a liar, you make it sound like today is my last day. That's not even close to what I am saying. You cannot do anything about yesterday; it's gone, you cannot work a day in the future because it hasn't arrived, but you can implement your ideas, strategies, and plans today for the future. We all should plan for tomorrow and the future, but you can never live in it until it becomes today.

Take the time today to do your best and be the best you possible. Don't waste another second procrastinating, making excuses, and watching others experience the life you desire. You have what it takes to get the job done and to live an exceptional life today.

Time is an Investment

We all have twenty-four hours each day, but we all don't spend our time the same. Due to some unfortunate circumstances, some of us may have less time to do things that others do. Some spends hours getting necessary treatment to help them stay alive. Others have loved ones who need their attention, which takes away from personal time to get things done. These people are doing what's most important to them. How about you? What's eating up your time? Is it things to help keep you or a loved one alive or is it something that's causing you to waste away your precious life?

Time is an investment! We get higher returns when we spend it wisely. Ask yourself, "What's the most valuable use of my time?" You should spend the majority of your time accomplishing the purpose for which you were born. Everything in your life should revolve around your life's assignment. Why? Because your life's assignment is the purpose for which God created you. Why would you spend most of your time doing something other than what the Creator created you to do? You were created for a purpose and fulfilling it doesn't happen automatically. In order to fulfill your purpose, you must use your time wisely. Time is an investment! Learn to value and manage your time. When you do, it becomes an investment into your future. There's no greater return on an investment than when you use your time to fulfill your purpose. It pays dividends spiritually, physically, mentally, and often financially.

Try to identify anything that hinders you from pursuing and fulfilling your life's purpose. Once you have identified it, you must eliminate it. The longer you wait the more time you waste and the longer it takes to feel gratified by accomplishing your life's assignment. Identifying your hindrances will be the easy part, but eliminating them can be a struggle for some. You'd be surprised at the things you think are beneficial that's actually stealing your time, joy, finances, and your destiny fulfillment.

Here's a short list of some things that's working against you and stealing valuable time from you:

Working unnecessary overtime - Instead of working unnecessary overtime, learn to become more productive in less time. This is one of the fastest ways to get a promotion or income increase. If you do more in less time, you save the organization money. Saved money can be increase for you.

Working a second job just for spending money - This one gets under my skin more often than not. I see too many people lose out on life and their purpose because they decided they needed a second job so they can spend more money on stuff that's doesn't matter. If they spent that amount of time working on their life's assignment, it's a good chance all their needs would be met plus money to spend.

Social media that's not being used as an advancement tool - Social media for personal use can be a big distraction and a waste of precious time. It is good when it is used to stay in contact with friends and loved ones. But to sit there for hours strolling to be nosey as well as posting pictures of your meal, new shoes, your pet, and so on is ridiculous. People should use that time to pull themselves out of the slums, debt, mediocre living, and life's frustrations. Again, I'm not against social media when it's used as a tool for relational, financial, or spiritual advancement.

People who don't value their time nor yours - People who don't value time will pop up, call, and text you whenever they feel like it. They are not concerned about what you are doing; they are only concerned with talking about things that have little to no value. It seems like they only call when you are trying to get something done. I know this may be a coincidence, but it seems as though they planned it. They call late when you are resting. They call early when you are trying to get that last few minutes of sleep. They call when you are on the phone handling business. They call while you are at church and you've told them tons of times not to call you on Sunday or Bible Study evenings. They are a distraction and you should handle them appropriately. I don't have this problem much because I have made it clear that I hate wasting time and I don't need friends who distract me or steal time from me. Value my time as I also try to value yours.

Watching Television - Watching television is not bad if you manage the amount of time you do it. Some of us can't afford to spend hours watching someone else's vision. That's what television is. It's telling us someone else's vision and we flop down and spend hours engulfed in it instead of working our vision. Calculate the amount of time you watch television and see what you could accomplish spending the same amount of time working on your life's assignment. Designate a certain amount of time for television enjoyment and then turn it off. I record the things I watch to eliminate having to watch all the commercials, even though I love commercials. I find them more amusing than the shows on television. I record because I save myself approximately 10 minutes for a 30-minute show and approximately 20 minutes for an hour show. Great time to work on my life's assignment.

The Nosey Neighbor - We all have some great neighbors that we would do whatever is possible for them and we feel they would do the same for us. But we also have that neighbor who doesn't have anything else to do but wait for you to step outside so they can bombard you with the latest community news. They talk to you so they can pass what you say to the next neighbor. Love them and treat them with respect, but don't allow them to make you their garbage can and dump trash on you. You have better things to do.

Being a "Yes" man or woman - A "yes" man or woman is someone who struggles with saying no to others. They always agree with people in order to not offend or to try to gain favor with them. This is a dangerous way of life. Everyone doesn't have the same moral values as you. Saying yes to them could compromise your moral values.

This is a short list of some things that can work against you and steal valuable time from you. There's many more, but I'll leave those for another book.

CHAPTER 9

GET YOUR HEAD IN THE GAME

I remember when I was younger, I played several different sports. Even though they were all different, there was one thing they all had in common. My coaches would all say, "Get your head in the game." For a long time, I didn't really grasp what that meant. I thought it meant to simply pay attention to the game. But now I understand it meant much more than to just pay attention. It meant to focus, be prepared, think before you get the ball, be in the right position, fundamentals before being flashy, know your opponent, be ready to assist your teammates, stay in tune with your coaches, and pay attention to the game. With that in mind, I say to you, "Get your head in the game!"

Your Focus Determines Your Energy

What you focus on determines your energy. Tony Robbins says it like this: "Energy flows where attention goes." Focus on the vision or goal and you will find the energy to do what's necessary to bring them to past. When you learn to focus, you begin to see things that you never saw before. Opportunities, opened doors, and favor are created when you focus your attention on the right things. Things that weren't available to you before becomes available when you focus on the vision and goal at hand. It's amazing how one little simple change can turn your situation and life around for the better.

There's a story about an old Cherokee Indian who is teaching his grandson about life. "A battle is going on inside each of us," he tells his grandson. "It's a terrible fight between two strong wolves. One wolf is evil. The other is good." The grandson thinks about this for a minute. Then he asks his grandfather, "Which one wins?" The wise old Cherokee answers, "The one you feed." This may be a good story to tell, but there's a ton of truth to it. What you feed grows. What you starve dies.

What you Feed Grows and What you Starve Dies

If you want increase in your life, feed the things that cause increase and starve the things that don't. The areas in your life that you desire to grow, feed them the necessary nutrients for growth. If you desire to walk in more faith, feed your mind scriptures on faith. If healing is your desire, then feed yourself scriptures on healing. By doing this, you are starving doubt and causing it to die. It works like plants, animals, and humans. Feed them, they will grow, starve them and they will die. As a child, I often wondered why farmers fed hogs the way they did. It appeared to me that the hogs were bad pets because all they did was stand around and eat. I had no idea that the farmer's sole purpose for feeding the hogs was to fatten them up, then kill them for food and money. He was feeding them so they would grow. It was years later that I came to understand the hogs were not the farmer's pet, but his meal and money.

Leaders learn to focus on the things that they want to grow and spend little time focusing on other things. Leaders think about their desired outcome and then find a way to achieve it. Think end results and you will find a way to get there. Our brains are very powerful organs. Just like a computer, our brain has a search function, but it is much more powerful than a computer. Our brains are programmed by what we focus on and what we identify with. I know it's hard to believe but when we focus and create a picture in our minds of what we really want, our minds automatically go to work to find a way to achieve it.

Trash or Treasure?

There's an old saying that makes a lot of sense. "Trash in, trash out." If we allow trash to get in our heads, trash will come out of our mouths and we will produce trashy results.

Have you ever been around someone who was supposed to be cleaning their house, but they only moved the trash from one spot to another? They never really cleaned; they just moved mess from one room to the next. This is very frustrating because they are only prolonging the inevitable. The trash must be taken out! For our minds to be renewed, we must take the trash out. We simply can't just move it from one place in our minds to the next. To renew our minds, we must clean out bad religion, old bad traditions, and the old unsuccessful way of thinking and doing things.

3 Ways to deal with trash

1. **Reuse as is** (Not recommended) Don't take old, bad trash and recirculate it. It's unhealthy, unacceptable, and disgusting. Nothing good ever comes out of recirculating bad, stinking trash. That's where we get stinking thinking from. Stinking thinking is recirculating things we've heard that have nor adds value to you or others.

2. **Reduce** (Use less or receive less trash) Trash will always come. You can't stop a thought from coming, but you can choose not to think on it. We may not be able to stop trash from coming but we can reduce it to a minimum.

3. **Recycle** (Best and most recommended) By recycling, you turn old products into new. You turn old, bad thinking into fresh new beneficial thinking. When something is recycled, it is treated or processed, but reusable. You are taking an old product and making it new.

(Romans 12:1)

I beseech you therefore, brethren, by the mercies of God, that ye present your bodies a living sacrifice, holy, acceptable unto God, which is your reasonable service.

(Romans 12:2)

And be not conformed to this world: but be ye transformed by the renewing of your mind, that ye may prove what is that good, and acceptable, and perfect, will of God.

Trash is worthless, discarded materials or objects: worthless or offensive material; empty words or ideas. So, if we are going to reuse trash, we must take the worthless, discarded, empty words and ideas and process/recycle them with the Word of God so our minds can be renewed and then we will know the good, acceptable, and perfect will of God.

7 truths about trash

1. Trash doesn't leave by itself.
2. Trash can cause health problems.
3. If you leave trash too long, it will start to stink. It must be taken out on a regular basis.
4. No one really wants to be around trash.
5. Trash as is has little to no value.
6. Trash packs itself on top of other trash.
7. Everyone contributes to the accumulation of trash. A little here and a little there.

Wouldn't be wonderful if trash just leaves on its own? All the men say Amen! But unfortunately, this is not how it works. Trash in our home and in our minds doesn't leave on its own; we must remove it. I was looking on the Internet and noticed an automatic vacuum cleaning machine. It just goes around on its own and vacuums the floor. Then I saw a lawn mower that's automatic as well. We even have cars now that drive on their own. Though I haven't seen it yet, but I'm wondering is there an automatic trash remover that's takes your trash out of your home on its own. Wouldn't that be nice? Even if everything we can think of becomes automatic, removing trash out of our minds will never be one of those things. It's not the way God made us. We must be deliberate about getting the old out and putting the new in.

Not understanding how to deal with trash is detrimental to leaders. If you want to mistreat good, innocent people, become a trashcan where others dump their thoughts and opinions on you about those people. The simple fact that you are reading this book tells me that this is not your intention. Though it may not be your intention, you are not exempt from falling into this trap. The best thing you can do is to eliminate or recycle all trash and refuse to become a trashcan.

Leading people is more enjoyable when you refuse to allow trash to become your determining factor. As I stated earlier, everybody has trash, but it's what you do with it that matters. Not everyone with trash are bad or evil people. For some it's a way of life. This is all they know. They were raised that way and don't know how to live any other way. This is where you come in. With your leadership skills and abilities, you should be able to help them identify and hopefully eliminate or recycle the trash that they deal with.

Here are a few simple tips that will help people identity and hopefully eliminate or recycle the trash that they deal with:

1. Identify whether it's trash or not. Someone's trash is another's treasure.
2. See what needs to be recycled and what needs to be eliminated.
3. Eliminate everything that doesn't deserve your attention.
4. Turn spilled milk into a milkshake. Whatever happened, happened! Past tense! Make the best of the situation.
5. Recycle the things through the Word of God that needs refocusing.
6. Focus on the things that are true, honest, pure, just, lovely, and of a good report.
7. Move on with your life with a fresh new perspective only looking ahead.

Treasure in the Midst of Trash

If you are like me, I have found some very valuable things in the midst of trash. I know it doesn't sound right, but it's true. I found lost jewelry, money, important papers, and other things as well. But the funny thing is, they were all found in what was supposed to be trash. Be careful not to discard your treasure that comes along with some trash. Though some people come with trash, listen carefully before you discard them because in the middle of the trash may be a treasure. I have found life changing nuggets in the same conversation of disgusting trash. Unfortunately, as a leader, there are times when you will have to listen to trash in order to get to the treasure. The very first words spoken to me by someone who played a major role in me becoming who I am was very offensive and I had to rule it as trash and discard it. It wasn't long afterward that the words they spoke to and about me became a life's treasure. As leaders we must endure hardness like a soldier.

2 Timothy 2:3

"Thou therefore endure hardness, as a good soldier of Jesus Christ."

Growing up, if we ate something or put something in our mouths that we shouldn't have, the older generation would say, "What don't kill you will make you fat." I never did get the full understanding of the quote, but I'm still alive and I do have several pounds of unwanted fat. So, I guess the quote means if you eat something that doesn't kill you the worst thing can happen is you get fat. While this is not totally true, it does go well with my next quote. "If the trash doesn't kill you then search it for treasure." In other words, sometimes we leaders must dig through the weeds to locate one healthy plant that has the ability to produce a large harvest. You've heard this saying before, "A diamond in the rough." There are people who are full of trash (unhealthy and ungodly language and lifestyle though **they are not trash**) that are actually diamonds. They need to be discovered, uncovered, then polished and refined to become what they were ordained to be.

CHAPTER 10

YOU ARE A TREASURE

There is an old saying, "One man's trash is another man's treasure." I take this to mean that something that carries no value to one can be of great value to another. Never underestimate your value to others even if you are told you are not valuable. Sometimes it takes people longer to recognize a treasure than it does trash. Trash is everywhere, all around us, all the time. On the other hand, treasures are hard to come by and can be easily overlooked. You are a treasure! In the previous chapter I shared three ways we deal with trash, now I want you to turn your attention to treasures.

6 things we do with treasures

1. We value our treasure.
2. We keep it safe.
3. We hold on to it.
4. We don't throw it away and we don't walk over or around it.
5. We don't move away from it.
6. We remain with our treasure regardless of how bad things get.

You are valued and you should be treated as such. If you are in a relationship where you are not valued, you should do all you can within reason to help them recognize your value. But if they absolutely refuse to value you it's probably best for you to seek God about leaving. If this relationship is a marriage then your focus should be on praying for them, loving them and treating them with value expecting to receive the same. I'm not an advocate for leaving your spouse unless it's under biblical terms.

Final Thoughts

SEE AND SEIZE THE OPPORTUNITY TO LEAD

Never allow an opportunity to lead to pass you by. I'm not saying take on every leadership role that's made available to you. But I am saying even if you refuse the position or title, still seize the opportunity to lead. Every good leader need team members who are willing to lead without a title or position. Anytime you see an opportunity to take the lead on something that's not out of God's will for you, seize that opportunity. Many times, God will use that opportunity to fine tune you for a greater one that's in the making. Joseph led his father's sheep before he led Israel. The task may appear small to you, but God has a larger plan for you, and you need to See and Seize that Opportunity for Leadership!

I believe this book has helped prepare you to take the next step in life and leadership. Don't stuff it on the bookshelf in the midst of all the other books with dust on them. Keep it close by and read it over and over again. Now go ahead and take the next leadership step by purchasing a copy for a friend or loved one. If this book helped you, it would definitely help them. God Bless and see you at the top!

jeffreyjames.info

For more books published by this author.